can you choo choo too?

david wojtowycz

little ORCHARD

Nee-nar nee-nar
Police cars dash

nee-nar
nee-nar
nee-nar

nee-nar
nee-nar
nee-nar

Fire engines coming
Flash flash flash

flash flash
flash
flash

zippety zoom

Plane goes whee
Zippety zoom

Super fast car
Brmm brmm vroom

brmm
vroom
brmm

Helicopters whirring
Whizzy-whizz

whizzy-whizz

Rocket blasting
whoosh whoosh fizz

whoosh

fizz

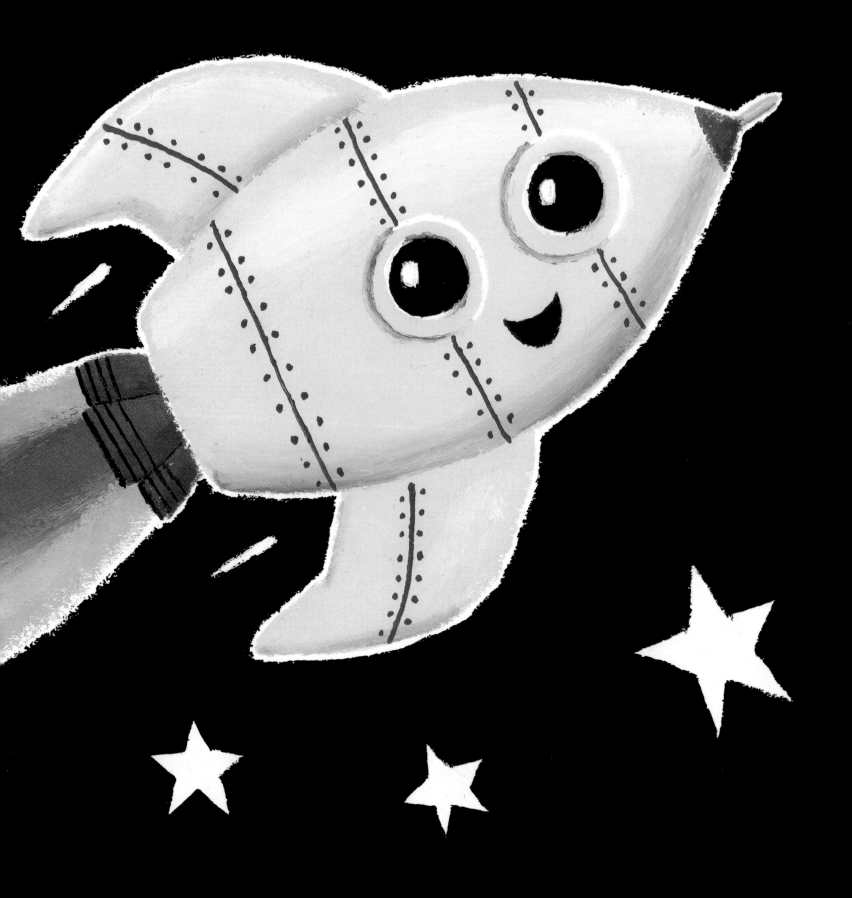

squish

Tractors squelching

squish
squish
squosh

Squish squish squosh

Little boat sailing
Splish splash splosh

splosh

Beep beep
Bus shiny and new

beep
beep
beep
beep

Clickety-clack train
Choo choo choo

choo choo ch

Noisy noises all around!

zippety zoom

choo choo choo choo choo

beep beep beep

vroom

brmm brmm

splish splash splosh

For Choo Choo Ciutto
and Mad Malin!
D.W

To my favourite nephew and
nieces, Jack, Poppy and Lilly
J.L

choo choo choo choo

With thanks to Ruby Lumley Godfree whose rmmm rmmm,
hoo hoo and plish plash helped inspire this book –
Jemima Lumley

ORCHARD BOOKS
96 Leonard Street, London EC2A 4XD
Orchard Books Australia
Unit 31/56 O'Riordan Street, Alexandria, NSW 2015
First published in Great Britain in 2001
ISBN 1 84121 036 6
Copyright © David Wojtowycz 2001
The right of David Wojtowycz to be identified as the author and
illustrator of this work has been asserted by him in accordance
with the Copyright, Designs and Patents Act, 1988.
A CIP catalogue record for this book is available from
the British Library
10 9 8 7 6 5 4 3 2 1
Printed in Singapore